I wanna be FAMOUS

For Cathie and Brian
for making it possible

An Angus & Robertson Publication

Angus&Robertson, an imprint of
HarperCollins*Publishers*
25 Ryde Road, Pymble, Sydney, NSW 2073, Australia
31 View Road, Glenfield, Auckland 10, New Zealand

First published in Australia in 1993
Book Club edition 1993
This Bluegum paperback edition published in Australia in 1994

National Library of Australia
Cataloguing-in-Publication data:

Whatley, Bruce.
  I wanna be famous.
  ISBN 0 207 18051 2 hbk
  ISBN 0 207 18150 0 pbk
  I. Title.
A823.3

Printed in Hong Kong
6 5 4 3 2
97 96 95 94

I wanna be FAMOUS

BRUCE WHATLEY

Angus&Robertson
An imprint of HarperCollins*Publishers*

'What do you want to be
when you grow up?' Dad asks.

'I wanna be famous,' I say.

'Well, that's great,' says Dad,
'but you have to do
something very special
to be famous.'

Dad drives a big crane
which loads giant containers onto ships.

That's special.

Perhaps I could be the best crane driver
in the world.

But I have trouble carrying the groceries.
I'll never be any good with giant containers.

Anyway, who's ever heard of
a famous crane driver?

Mum's a very good gardener.
Dad says she has green fingers.

Unfortunately, when I try gardening,
my fingers just go a dirty brown.
So does the rest of me.

I'll never be a famous gardener.

My big sister wants to be a doctor
when she grows up.

I nearly faint at the sight of my blood.
When I fall off my bike and graze my knee,
she does a great job of bandaging me up.

I don't think I want to be a famous doctor.

My baby brother just
eats and sleeps.
I'm very good at both of these.

But who wants to be famous
for being the fattest,
laziest person in the world?

There must be something else.

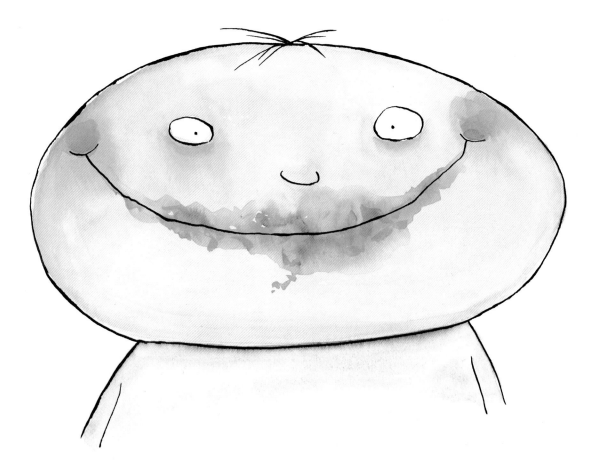

My best friend Roger wants to be a fireman
when he grows up.

Roger likes climbing ladders and
he's a great shot with his water pistol.

I would have to climb a very big ladder
to be a famous fireman.

I *hate* heights.

I could be a famous movie star.

I'll be recognised wherever I go.
My fans will chase me for my autograph
and the girls will probably hug and kiss me.

Er yuk, I don't think I want to be
a famous movie star!

Perhaps I could be a famous archaeologist.

My teacher tells us about
pyramids and tombs full of treasure,
unopened for thousands of years.

'They must find lots of cobwebs too,' I say.

'Yes, spiders *and* snakes,' says Mr Lewis.

Spiders I don't mind, at a distance,
but snakes?

No thank you!

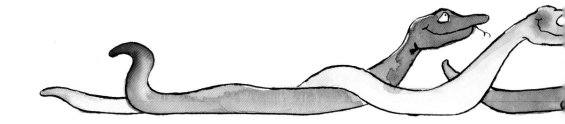

I love making my lunch.
Maybe I could become a famous chef.

Though Mum does say
my double-decker strawberry jam,
salami and cold chip sandwich
with salad and tomato sauce
is going a bit too far.
And that I am the only one
in the world who would eat it.

I'll never be a famous chef
if nobody will eat my food.

I know. I'm a good soccer player.
We always play after lunch.

Roger kicks the ball to Tim.

Tim heads the ball to Susie,
who sends a lovely pass to me.
I swerve around Derek
and line up for the perfect goal.

This is it. My moment of glory.

Billy comes from nowhere
with a monster of a tackle…

BOOMPH!

Guess I'll never be a famous soccer player.

Maybe I could be an inventor.

Today, in science, we experiment with jet propulsion. There must be lots of extraordinary things like that I could invent…

BANG!

I guess you have
to concentrate really hard
to be a famous inventor.

I have trouble concentrating sometimes.

I'll have to do something really special
if I am going to be famous.
I don't seem to be really good at anything.

On my way home from school I see
my baby brother climbing our tree.
He'll probably end up
being a famous mountain climber.

But he isn't supposed to be doing that.
'Hey Billy, *STOP!* You'll fall!' I shout.
But Billy keeps on climbing.

I drop my school bag and run faster
than I've ever run before.

I leap over Mrs Denton's sleepy dog,
side-step Mr Spiro who's painting his front gate,
vault over Mr Lamb's rubbish bin
and dive under the tree
just as Billy loses his balance…

'That's the bravest thing
I've ever seen,' someone says.

It's a cameraman from the TV station.
He's there to film Mum's prize roses.

'I'm going to show that
on the news tonight,' he says.

Mum races over and
gives us both a big hug.

That night we all sit around the TV.

It's very exciting.
Mum and Dad are very proud.
My sister thinks it's really cool.
Billy wonders what all the fuss is about.

'I don't even have to wait
until I grow up to be famous,' I say.

I'm famous for just being myself.